# Story

I can read the Speed sounds.

I can read the Green words.

I can read the Red words.

I can read the story.

I can answer the questions about the story.

I can read the Speed words.

# Story 1 Tug, tug

## Say the Speed sounds

### Consonants

*Ask your child to say the sounds (not the letter names) clearly and quickly, in and out of order. Make sure he or she does not add 'uh' to the end of the sounds, e.g. 'f' not 'fuh'.*

| f | l ll | m | n | r | s | v | z | sh | th | ng nk |
|---|---|---|---|---|---|---|---|---|---|---|
|   |   |   |   |   |   |   |   |   |   |   |

| b | c k ck | d | g | h | j | p | qu | t | w | x | y | ch tch |
|---|---|---|---|---|---|---|---|---|---|---|---|---|
|   |   |   |   |   |   |   |   |   |   |   |   |   |

*Each box contains one sound.*

## Vowels

*Ask your child to say each vowel sound and then the word, e.g. 'a', 'at'.*

| at | hen | in | on | up | day | see | high | blow | zoo |
|---|---|---|---|---|---|---|---|---|---|

## Read the Green words

*For each word ask your child to read the separate sounds, e.g. 'f-a-t', 'f-i-sh' and then blend the sounds together to make the word, e.g. 'fat', 'fish'. Sometimes one sound is represented by more than one letter, e.g. 'sh', 'th', 'ck'. These are underlined.*

ca<u>tch</u>    fat    sat    wi<u>ll</u>    fi<u>sh</u>    big

yes    <u>th</u>en    rod    and

*Ask your child to read the root word first and then the word with the ending.*

fi<u>sh</u> → fi<u>sh</u>ing    <u>ch</u>ip → <u>ch</u>ips

## Read the Red words

*Red words don't sound like they look. Read the words out to your child. Explain that he or she will have to stop and think about how to say the red words in the story.*

he    s<u>ai</u>d    no    I

# Tug, tug

**Introduction**

*Black Hat Bob is fishing in his boat. He is looking forward to eating a lovely supper of fish and chips.*

Black Hat Bob got his fishing rod.

"I will catch a big fat fish," he said.
"Fish and chips - yum!"

**Ask your child:**
⭐ *Why does Black Hat Bob want to catch a fish?*

7

He sat . . .

and he sat . . .

# No big fish.

Then . . . tug tug

"Yes . . . a fish!" said Black Hat Bob.

tug tug

"Hmmm!"

**Ask your child:**
⭐ What does Black Hat Bob catch on his rod?

11

# Speed words for Story ⭐1

*Ask your child to read the words across the rows, down the columns and in and out of order, clearly and quickly.*

| catch | fat | sat | will | fish |
|-------|-----|-----|------|------|
| then | big | his | hat | he |
| said | no | I | and | rod |
| got | fishing | yum | yes | chips |

# Story

I can read the Speed sounds.

I can read the Green words.

I can read the Red words.

I can read the story.

I can answer the questions about the story.

I can read the Speed words.

# Story ⟨2⟩ The web

## Say the Speed sounds

### Consonants

*Ask your child to say the sounds (not the letter names) clearly and quickly, in and out of order. Make sure he or she does not add 'uh' to the end of the sounds, e.g. 'f' not 'fuh'.*

| f | l<br>ll | m | n | r | s | v | z | sh | th | ng<br>nk |
|---|---|---|---|---|---|---|---|---|---|---|

| b | c<br>k<br>ck | d | g | h | j | p | qu | t | w | x | y | ch |
|---|---|---|---|---|---|---|---|---|---|---|---|---|

*Each box contains one sound.*

### Vowels

*Ask your child to say each vowel sound and then the word, e.g. 'a', 'at'.*

| at | hen | in | on | up | day | see | high | blow | zoo |
|---|---|---|---|---|---|---|---|---|---|

## Read the Green words

*For each word ask your child to read the separate sounds, e.g. 's-p-i-n', 'p-i-nk' and then blend the sounds together to make the word, e.g. 'spin', 'pink'. Sometimes one sound is represented by more than one letter, e.g. 'ck', 'nk', 'th'. These are underlined.*

spin    six    stuck    black    pink

long    thin    them    munch    this

*Ask your child to read the word in syllables.*

can'not → cannot

*Ask your child to read the root word first and then the word with the ending.*

sit → sitting         bug → bugs

spot → spots         wing → wings

## Read the Red words

*Red words don't sound like they look. Read the words out to your child. Explain that he or she will have to stop and think about how to say the red words in the story.*

said    the    my    are

# Story 2
## The web

**Introduction**

A spider is sitting on his web, counting the bugs he has caught. Will he manage to eat them all?

This is Spin.

Spin is sitting in his web.

"Six bugs are stuck in my web," said Spin.

"A big black bug . . .

a bug with spots . . .

a flat pink bug . . .

**Ask your child:**
*How many bugs are stuck in Spin's web?*

18

a bug with six wings . . .

a fat red bug . . .

and a long thin bug."

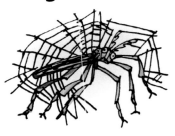

"I will get the six bugs and munch them up!"

But . . .

"I cannot stand up!"
said Spin.
"I am stuck in my web!"

**Ask your child:**
✿ *What has happened to Spin?*

# Speed words for Story 2

*Ask your child to read the words across the rows, down the columns and in and out of order, clearly and quickly.*

| | | | | |
|---|---|---|---|---|
| spots | spin | cannot | his | web |
| six | stuck | black | wings | flat |
| pink | fat | sitting | red | long |
| thin | them | up | munch | my |